Wendy Frood Auger
Art by Zsolt Mató

Literacy Consultants
David Booth • Larry Swartz

www.rubiconpublishing.com

Editorial Director: Amy Land
Project Editor: Dawna McKinnon
Creative Director: Jennifer Drew
Art Director: Rebecca Buchanan
Colorist: Irina Furin

Printed in Singapore

ISBN: 978-1-77058-561-4
6 7 8 9 10 11 12 13 14 15 2016 25 24 23 22 21 20 19 18 17 16
4500568932

Can Brandon survive the dangerous jungle journey?

CHARACTERS

Brandon is packing to go on a trip to Africa with his parents.
Brandon's parents are photographers, and they are going to take pictures of gorillas, zebras, and other wild animals.
Don't forget to pack your mosquito net hat. We'll be going deep into the jungle!

Good night! Sleep tight! Don't let the baboons bite!
Night, Dad.
Brandon drifts off to sleep ...

After a long flight, Brandon and his parents meet their jungle guide, Zama, at the airport.
ARRIVAL
It's great to meet you, Zama. This is our son Brandon.
Hi, Brandon. Are you ready for a real jungle journey?

Let's head out to camp. We've got a long day ahead of us.
On the way to camp, they see some interesting animals.
Wow! This is so cool!
Wait until you see all of the beautiful animals in the jungle!
After a long and bumpy ride, they arrive at the campsite.
This is it! We should start setting up camp before it gets dark.

Everyone chips in to help.
Hey, Brandon. Want to come with me to find some wood for a campfire?
Sure!

We have to be very careful when —
What was that?
RUSTLE! RUSTLE!
Shhh! Just keep very quiet and still.

What is it, Dad?
It's an African golden cat! We hope to photograph one of these!
When the cat leaves, Brandon and his dad head back to camp.
Later that night ...
... and it was RIGHT THERE!
Tomorrow's going to be a big day! We'd better get some rest.

The next morning...
We have to travel down the river to the spot where the gorillas gather. We'll get some great shots!
We're going on the raft? Cool!

A few hours later, Brandon is hot and bored, when...
According to the map, we just have to go around this —

BEND!
Hold on tight!
Almost there!
Whoa! Ahhhhh!
ZAMA!
Brandon and his parents are relieved when they finally make it to shore.
Wasn't that fun?
Oh yeah, Zama.
A real blast!

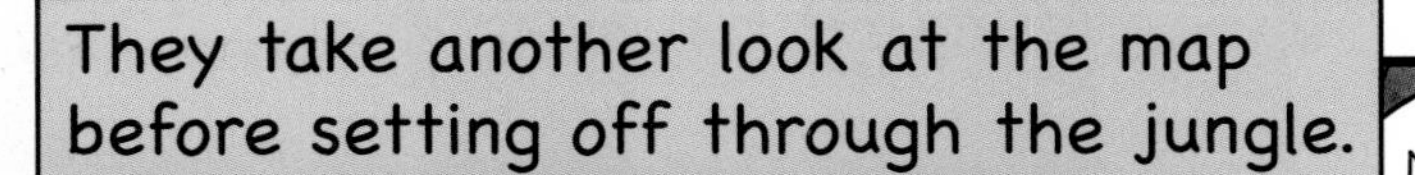
They take another look at the map before setting off through the jungle.

Incredible! It's a bush baby — one of the smallest primates. It's very rare to see one during the day.
Once the sun sets, it will go looking for food and hang out with other —
GRWWWWLLLLL!
WHAT WAS THAT?

I don't know, but I don't want to stick around to find out!
Brandon, his parents, and Zama slowly sneak away from the area.
Phew! That was close! I don't know what it was, but it did not sound happy!
A few minutes later, the group draws close to the gorillas.
Almost there, folks!

Be VERY careful! We're walking through the home of the green mamba — one of the most dangerous snakes in the world.
The g-g-green mamba?
Yes, they live in the trees and they —

AHHHHHHHHHHH!
SNAAAAKE!
Suddenly, everything is dark and quiet.
Brandon sees two scary glowing eyes.
MEOW!

Morning, champ!
Ready for your jungle journey?
The plane leaves in
two hours!
Jungle journey?
But, we've already —

I'm ready, all right!

Comprehension Strategy: Summarizing

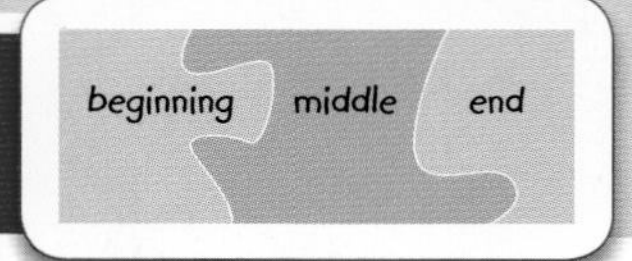

Common Core Reading Standards

Foundational Skills

4c. Use context to confirm or self-correct word recognition and understanding, rereading as necessary.

Literature

3. Describe how characters in a story respond to major events and challenges.
5. Describe the overall structure of a story
6. Acknowledge differences in the points of view of characters
9. Compare and contrast two or more versions of the same story (e.g., Cinderella stories) by different authors

Reading Foundations

Word Study: Contractions

High-Frequency Words: animal, around, beautiful, better, cat, dad, everyone, head, home, hours, leaves, night, pictures, sleep

Reading Vocabulary: Africa, camp, flight, gorilla, journey, jungle, parents, snake, tomorrow, travel, trip

Fluency: Changing Voice to Reflect Characters

BEFORE Reading

Prereading Strategy Making Connections

- Introduce the book by showing the cover and reading the title aloud. Say: *Let's make a text-to-world connection. The setting of this story is a jungle. Can you relate to this setting?*

Introduce The Comprehension Strategy

- Point to the Summarizing visual on the inside front cover of this book. Say: *Today we will summarize. Summarizing means using your own words to retell only the most important ideas and events in a book.*
- Write the following on the board: *Meg was nervous about the test. Meg scratched her ear. Meg studied hard. Meg dropped her pencil. Meg passed the test.*

  Modeling Example Say: *Every story and every summary should have a beginning, middle, and end. I have written the events of a story so we can practice summarizing.* Read the sentences. *First, I pick out the most important events. I don't think that scratching an ear or dropping a pencil is important so I will delete those details. Now I can summarize.*
- Draw a three-column chart on the board. Label the columns *Beginning*, *Middle*, and *End*. Under *Beginning* write: *Meg was nervous about the test.* Under *Middle* write: *, but she studied hard.* Under *End* write: *and passed it.*
- Say: *Good readers summarize because it helps us understand the main events in the texts we read. Summaries should be as short as possible.*